Summer Holds Too Long

&

Rooting

ISBN 1-55780-099-5
Juniper Book 52

Summer Holds Too Long

By

Leslie Crutchfield Tompkins

Juniper Press
La Crosse, WI

ACKNOWLEDGMENTS

Some of these poems appeared first in the
following publications: *Pembroke Magazine, Uwharrie
Review, Intersections, Sing, Heavenly Muse!* and *Northeast.*
"Chiaroscuro" will appear in *The New Renaissance #25* in
spring, 1988.
"Thinning Into Fall" will appear in
Southern Poetry Review.

for Julie Suk

"On the door it tells you what to do to survive
But we were not born to survive
Only to live"

W.S. Merwin
"Keeper of the Bees"

and in memory of Gloria

STILL LIFE

Thin pines hold
black crosshatch
against white noon.
Chickens pose
before scratching gravel.
The hound fixes
on a petrified cat.

Inside the barn
dust stipple hangs
in broken sun.
Brittle spiders stick
to old webs.
Here it could be years
before anything moves.

CONTENTS

CHIAROSCURO

That last flush of amber
just before dusk,
the sudden hesitancy
of warm before cool,
color backing into shadow
and once hidden,
its reluctance to be named.
Leonardo was right:
the light in late afternoon
is for painting the human face.

IN ANOTHER COUNTRY

Sorry. Thought I recognized
landmarks in your face,
felt familiar contours
along the bones of your hand,
caught a cry that tore
in flight across your voice.
Forgive me for staring.
Someone I knew
once lived there.

WITHOUT LINES

In painting class I learned
nature has no lines,
only edges, and those can blur.
This is not enough.
The eye demands horizon,
needs to see the end
of white space,
the place where sky begins.
All I know is that it's hard
to draw my own profile
against the wide face of winter,
easy to lose color to the blizzard.
And I protest,
protest until the frozen breath
outlines my head.

TO TAKE NOTE OF

You tell me to forget, move on,
make a new life.
I remember the day we buried
a wild rabbit outside our window,
found a small stone marker,
one that said yes,
here, this spot near the tree.

And if the tree is one day gone,
hardly a trace of roots,
this will still be the place
of something lost,
buried in a flower bed
now wild in weeds.

BY OWNER

It's not what she says—
she says the right things.
It's her eyes, a look.
One sweep
takes my whole backyard:
azaleas, tool shed, porch.
She is first to notice
a tree fallen on the power line
down by the creek—
her creek, her tree,
her power line.

THE MOVERS

Tramping through the house,
thieves handle my past:
shaking its print from the rug,
its bouquet from a drawer,
muffling its tone in a quilt
and heaving it up on the truck.
Decisions and beds
once carefully made
now come apart.
Impatient, a van waits
to close doors.
"The insurance, lady—
what value?"

Afternoon sun
slanting leaf patterns
on a pale kitchen wall.
Voices rising in the stairwell.
This shaft of dust motes—
years of words
left hanging.

PRONOUN SHIFTS

Perhaps I've passed you on the street.
Maybe you and I brushed in some hall,
smiled in an elevator, polite,
the way we are with strangers.
You must have been
one of those smart young women in suits
who pursue their work seriously,
the kind men appreciate
because their wives don't understand,
the kind who go find coffee.
How you must have smiled at him
over lunches, bravely smiled
when he asked how you managed
a full-time job and raising kids alone.

He dines at your house now.
Not guessing you, I watched
while ours caved in—leaving a haze
of his, yours, mine.
We clean up, redecorate—
the civilized way to handle remains.
Change pictures, shift a few chests,
a few children.

I am careful these days
not to turn my head at counters
or nod to those next to me in line.
I'd know the face, the smile.

SOLSTICE

I'd hoped someone would come
sit with me on the stoop
and have a fudgesicle.
Or we could sit in chairs out back,
maybe even walk around the block,
if it weren't for gnats
after all this rain.
Oh, there are things that need doing—
supper dishes, the shirts,
the dry ferns.
It's just that after supper,
everyone leaves.
I need my lemonade sweetened.
I could have company—
and would, if the ferns weren't dying.
I'd have to explain about the ferns,
how I let that happen.

SEARS GARDEN SHOP

The cashier has the answer.
"That ad is two weeks old.
This week it's lime on special."
Her laugh is not unkind.

I came for decorative bark.
At the other house, remember—
or was it finer bark we always used
around the birdbath. Pine straw,
get pine straw. What does lime do.

The cashier stays in one place.
She talks about a three-piece suit
she's bought her son for Easter.
It took her months to pay.

Why does it have to be Easter—
I haven't done a thing
about Easter—I should buy mine a shirt
or something. This week it's lime.
I need decorative bark.

(continued)

Her eyes are not unkind.
She's off at five. It's Good Friday.
She won't get drunk, she laughs,
but plans to have a few.

I dread five, dread moving
away from that laugh.
I want to ask her things. Tell me.
Tell me how to live.
The soil is acid here.

ENTRANCES AND EXITS

I used to live here.
Here we planted roses
where you could see them
from the porch. Here we added on,
measured our way
through a wall, a door,
grew shelves for books and toys.
Miraculously, the new room
arrived before the baby.
It took days to choose a name,
weeks to decide on paint.
For eight years
the boys played army by the creek
while I failed at Hybrid Peace.

When we moved on,
the next couple brought a desk
that filled up my new room.
They saw possibilities
in the yard, stayed eight years.
When they moved out,
she was crying in the back.
Her boys had played by the creek,
and she had planted azaleas.

(continued)

Now music I don't know
beats from the kichen sill.
A young couple sips beer
in the room they paint loud green.
"Sure. Come in. Look around."
Flipping on the hall light,
she dances back to chartreuse trim
and toys with the idea of babies.
She is surprised I exist.

She doesn't know
about the hall light,
how I bought it on sale,
how it made me feel
like a good wife.
She doesn't know about the roses,
how long they took to kill.

OF THE JEWELWEED FAMILY

I was planting Impatiens—
digging, filling, pressing,
hiding my hands in work—
when you came by.
And I could feel you watching
for the ring, the absence,
that same unfocused look
you often fixed.
I could feel you seeing
my hands,
fingers spread like a child's
but far from childhood now,
these hands
two strangers, bare.

MY BROTHER'S KEEPER

My brother and I could hear
Betsy Hamilton practice piano
in a house with polished doorknobs,
hear her on our walk home from school,
all the way to the corner of Belvedere.
Her mother made her do it.
As far as I knew, there was no father,
or need for one. In their yard,
ligustrum practiced restraint.

My brother lusted after Betsy
through grades five and six, lusted
for her pale, stringy hair, indoor legs
and skin you could see through.
In his jacket I found her picture, creased
between a Field Guide and muslin sack
for snakes she'd never touch.

He spent his hard-earned courage
on the telephone, told her she was beautiful.
I could have told her
it was the way a poplar by his window moved
against the moon on summer nights
that drove him longing,
pine's acrid sweet, a shrill pipe
of tree frogs, the nightbirds crying.
I could have told her it was the owl,
unattainable hoot owl,
he hung out the window for.

THE WAY BACK

Sometimes at night she sensed him
reading in the next room.
She'd feel her way, then remember
they'd taken his green chair.
Or she'd have an impulse to wait
before going out; he could find keys,
could see to set the thermostat.

It made her nervous to ask again
just who it was that died.
Now they'd brought her here.
This wasn't Aunt Edith's grave,
or her brother Randolph's.
She drew her past in, focused
while a nurse read the epitaph.

The old alertness flew to her face.
Bending by herself,
she touched the rough edge,
found his years,
traced the letters of his name.
She gave the stone
three light pats,
the way she would his knee.

HER GRAVE

Do not presume she
has gone to rest
,or roll your heavy peace
over her lightness.
Do not impose
the safe gladiola
in its hothouse pot.
She has no need
for order.
Let wild things go—
columbine run,
trumpet vines,
let dragonfly wings catch sun.

NOT LIKE HER

If I were blind and old,
I would not play the organ
for chapel service
or sing a blessing at dinner
or ask the nurse to read to me
about a boxing match.
Searching for the green of any leaf,
I would lie and glare
at my skull's white ceiling.
I would clench the knots of my hands,
beat against that white,
beat like the bird I once saw
fighting a glass door.

IF IN THAT HOUSE

From the street I try to remember
who lived in which house.
Wasn't that the Wilkinsons'—
the tree, last house by the field?
The one with facade gone bland,
windowboxes not planted.
Neglect has always depressed me.

By now they are old, Mr. Wilkinson
too frail to mow, Mrs. Wilkinson
no longer herself. I know
before asking: by now a nursing home,
apartment without a yard.
Afraid of yes, afraid of no,
a small, unruly sprig takes root,

a dreamer's hope, that somehow
the Wilkinsons still live in that house
where they are supposed to live—there
on my way to everywhere, there,
where my mother chased Benny Wilkinson
all the way home and up to his room
for poking a stick in my bicycle spokes.

During separation I dreamed fire
across this street,
dreamed I stood
in the Wilkinsons' yard—
ashes and charred stubble—my stick
poking for shade
in a still-smoking stump.

OR

I have definitely decided
the time has come to begin
thinking about starting
to come to a decision.

The time has come to begin
thinking about
starting to
come to
a decision to
decide to
not decide.

The time has come
to begin thinking
about starting
to come to
a decision about
deciding by
not.

RING AROUND THE MOON

Reach for those beside you
in the circle at nursery school.
Make sure they are there
before you sing.
Reach for a brass ring the man gave you
for staying on the painted horse
one more time around, and reach for
that other man, the gold band he gave,
then after many years,
took away.
Reach for the friend who died,
for friendships that went
when no one died at all.
Reach for children
as each one leaves.
Reach down
to a face in the water—
never mind a lifeline—
reach for her,
encircle her with your arms,
close the gap.

FUNERAL ANTHEM

In the chancel a new soprano
sings like the one who is missing,
whose death was quick,
headlights turned on her.
Notes dart high,
dive among the arches,
brushing antiphonal stone.

Once more the flying,
this hovering
before stained glass, flying
into the light,
into light
and out.

THINNING INTO FALL
For M L'E

September 1986

My eyes are fixed on the feeder.
The hummingbird has left the terrace,
deserted the flower pots,
abandoned his hanging bottle half full.
Perhaps the sweet red nectar
has grown too strong in the sun,
lacquered hibiscus too hot
against the bricks, this last burst
of honeysuckle, too late.

Brown tubers loosen
in the ground.
White on white, you fade
in a hospital bed,
sustained by transparent stems.

I wonder how much strength it takes
to keep on drawing,
how much it takes to turn
a long look back across the summer,
how fast the ebbed-down heart must beat
before it leaves.

THIS SUMMER HOLDS TOO LONG

Clothes hang limp
in the closet, tropical prints
that blossomed back in June.
Outside, a false summer,
enough crickets left to pretend.
Leaves feign at night
the same live green we remember,
rattle dull in the daylight.

There is such a thing as too much green,
old green choking all chance
of fall's true colors.
Heat we welcomed in freedom
hangs too close, gnats
no longer waved away with good grace.
And every day we walk the dog,
holding to the same route
in these same thin cottons.

Too hot to change, we say, ignoring
rich wools in that other closet—
half willing to feed them to the heat,
not believing in their textures
or the substance of their weight,
not trusting new colors,
how they shape us.

ABOUT THE AUTHOR

Leslie C. Tompkins of Charlotte, N.C., works in the Writing Center at Central Piedmont Community College there. After Connecticut College and UNC-Chapel Hill, her pursuit of the arts has expanded into a renewed love of music, always an essential in her life. She enjoys creating workshops which relate visual art, music, and literature. She is working on a collection of children's poems, exploring her own childhood and that of three grown sons.

Rooting

By

Lynne Hume Burgess

Juniper Press
La Crosse, WI

ACKNOWLEDGMENTS

Some of these poems appeared first in the following publications: *Alumni Poetry Center Journal of Boston University, Northeast,* and *Song.*

CONTENTS

LEAVE OF ABSENCE: A BALLAD

Leda leans over a stone wall
And stares at the valley below
Where, through carefully tended fields,
The silver rivers flow.

Her hands hold a fluttering plan book
Closed over ruler and pen.
A school bell rings; time is short,
The children approach again.

Leda turns her back to the valley
And starts to mark out her day,
But the rivers in her arteries swell
Against this ritual way.

The air grows still, the sun burns hot;
Leda stops to listen.
There is a smell of sour feathers,
The sound of gabbling and hissing.

A huge grey goose, big as a man,
Appears and comes down at her,
His head lowered, his wings spread out:
The day begins to tatter.

(Continued)

In a tumble of feathers she's tossed to his back
Like moss into a cauldron.
His muscles pull wings up and up;
Leda screams out, "Children!"

Then Leda lets her plan book fall,
There is no other choice.
Below, the valley's patterns fade,
And she sings with a gosling's voice.

LEGACY

Before Ansel died,
he told us where to find morels,
frail links between earth and air.
Under the gooseberry bush, he said,
near the dead elm.
He gave us his pitchfork, a calico cat,
and told us about the morels,
an old man's secret.
Under the gooseberry bush, he said,
near the dead elm.
But something shifted that warm spring,
and they were gone.
Still, each wet May,
we search for the paths of spawn and spore,
those sponge thumbs pressing up
through humus.
Our first stop is Ansel's elm.

MAKING HAY ON THEIR ANNIVERSARY

In four-wheel-drive low
they pull the wagon uphill
following the rattling baler
that spits out wrapped grass.
They sweat in the truck's cab
and find no relief
on the hot brown hillside.
It's stop, brakes straining,
heave the bales up
past unblinking sun
onto the rickety wagon.
Shirt and jeans soak
salt, eyes sting,
and skin is sticky with grit.
Words drop out
in the rhythm of brake, lift,
heave, thud, and breathe.
Again and again, pulling
against gravity, they work.
There is no quitting
until it's too dark to see.

ROOTING IN NOVEMBER

You dig. I pull at horseradish,
back bowed, legs tented over
frostbitten sagging leaves.
The root snaps, throws me back,
its white mouth shining, hot breath
blowing, and the redworms curl
and howl with rubbery laughter.
To think, to think!
We watch escaping roots rejoice
in wet sucking clods,
hairy fingers clutching hold,
staying on.
            In spring green flags
will wave to let us know that
horseradish runs deep
for all our well-meant harvest.

THE RETURN

I found the knife you lost;
It was in an ice cave
Not even rusty.

I follow a dog sled
Wind and snow blinding me.
That must be you, plunging ahead
Into the whiteness.
My toes are numb, and my face. . .
We're on our way home
From the South Pole.

The blankets have fallen off
My body aches from holding itself curled
Against the cold, sheets chilling limbs.
Then you sigh and roll over,
Tucking yourself along my curved back.
So we travel, skin and pulse warming,
the last few miles.

The knife handle fits my palm exactly.
I lay its cool blade against my cheek,
The edge cutting South.

AXIOMS

Two old people will need her
to hold the lantern
as they test a mountain's uncertain edge.
They worry about their footing.

Two women will climb the steps to a stone tower.
It will be icy, and they will slip off.
There will be no sound.
Another woman will watch, helpless.
The walled city will become
two-dimensional.

A boy will reach the windmill's rusting spokes.
His fall will be broken by a hand clasping
his belt.
He will survive.
The woman will need surgery on her wrist.

She will switch the lantern to her left hand.

REQUIEM FOR A HACKBERRY

There was a crack through the hackberry's heart.
No longer could it bear the weight of limbs
Reaching up and out, a pulling apart
At the core. Last winter's ice had wedged its arms
Still more, and the tree that shaded our way home
Was losing the strength to stand. Then chainsaw's whine
Left the wide stump's rings exposed and drove
Sawdust rivulets into the woods. "The pines
Will straighten now," you said. "They have the space
To grow." Making room for others. . . . is that
What death's about? And must we speed the race
When heart grows frail, the body's final fact?
      I looked above the morning's work to where
      The sun shown through an absence in the air.

BALANCING

A dull ache gathers in my swollen breasts.
It is dark and still, save for your steady breathing.
Moons, many of them, have come and, like this one, gone
With a sloughing of cells washed in familiar blood.
Still, the possibilities of this pain take me
To morning's edge where light and darkness balance:
A newborn stirs in a far away crib,
Her small mouth sucking, even in sleep. . . .
Then shadows shift, and I ride malignancy's end
To white tangled sheets, coiled plastic tubes,
And voices murmuring in a wide hallway.
In abdomen's center, at last, there is a twist,
And as the coming dawn begins to crest,
I pull your sleeping hand across my chest.

A Mothering

. . . after "Death with a Woman,"
woodcut by Käthe Kollwitz

It is touching the shell of a puffball, releasing
brown spore smoke into the air:

It is watching the cat crunch small bones of a mouse,
caught while suckling her young:

It is standing cornstalks up in shocks,
cobs stolen by the raccoon:

It is pulling warm innards out of the hen,
spilling yokes of unformed eggs, chicken soup boiling
on the woodstove all day, into the night:

It is my hand on your beard, my finger tracing
the lines that crest above your cheekbone, finding
the first silver hairs at your temple:

It is a mothering.

SINGING TO THE COMET

It has been dark, dark until this clear night.
Now, clouds dispersed, the waxing moon
Casts shadows past its light. Deep within
My cells, the moment reached, I wake,
Aware the time is right to scan the edge
of Cat Back Ridge for a tail among the faithful
Stars. I face toward a warm south wind
which, wrapping gown around my legs, draws me
Out into the whirling sky to seek
An emblem of our history, promising a future
I'll not be on this deck to see. And though
I cannot find the comet's hazy trail,
A certainty invades the moving night:
The universe contains its parabolic flight.

MAY

The aunts laughed raucously by the veranda. May caught the words "old maid" twisting up into the smoke above their gossip. Glasses clinked, Uncle Ned belched, and May's fingernails pressed hard into her fists. Family gatherings had begun to depress her.

It was time to get out. May's eyes met those of her Great Grandmother May, eyes that glowed, still and blue, from the darkened portrait that had always hung above the mantle. Hands seemed to reach toward her from her namesake's sober stare, hands that bound her, a barren branch, to the family tree.

"The spitting image," Cousin Joe said, breathing brandy into her face. How many times had she heard those moldy words? She had been May long enough. Seeds had swollen and withered in her tight womb for the last time. A spring wind blew past the organdy curtains and, on its crest, May thought she heard a baby's cry. It was time for her summer to begin.

After the smoke had been swished out the windows, the leaves drawn from the dining room table, and the last plate dried, they found her sitting in the wing-backed chair, illuminated by moonlight. Her skin was white, and there were purple circles under her eyes. She had loosened her hair so that it hung in brown waves down her chest.

"You're tired," they said. "Get some sleep." May nodded. She could hear the worry in their voices. "It isn't like her," she heard them mutter. When they left, May whispered, "Summer," into the moonlight,

"Summer." She felt the soil in her heart shift in preparation and knew her name was June.

Now June had to find a farmer to plant her fields. And there he was. In the front pew at church. Big Henry. Everyone called him that. He opened his arms and in she went, all but disappearing in his wide embrace. Big Henry laughed, and flesh tumbled in compex rhythms around his frame.

"Such corporeal promise," June thought. "I'll take him if, that is, there is a working planter under that huge belly." There was.

So June became July and produced Onion, her darling daughter of the red skin and white hair. Big Henry laughed and bounced the baby on his hills and valleys. Then came Bean and Kernel, the Peas, they called them. Henry put one on each shoulder and spun around and around until they all fell dizzy into the hay. July watched from the front window, her hands against the pane, the sunlight heating her blood, and felt herself become August. She always knew that it was at this moment she conceived Melon, by herself, so fertile was her summer body. One day as she rocked Melon under the apple tree, she looked down into the sober blue eyes and felt hands, familiar hands, reach up for her from the round white face with its tiny mouth. "May," echoed in the baby's cry. It was then she knew she had one more child to make.

September, for so she named herself now, called Big Henry in from the barn. He didn't object. Manure stained the sheets. September made him give her Root. It was a difficult birth. She had to reach in and pull the twisted brown body out, so hard did Root cling to her womb. In the harsh daylight, he squalled and moaned, keeping his eyes and fists clenched tight. "It is this baby that will hold me here, to this earth," September thought. "Now I am done." She hummed to Melon who was playing with the cat by the woodstove. Henry was trying to sooth the fussing Root with a sugary finger dipped in brandy.

Already the days were getting shorter. "Thanks, Big Henry," September said. "I'm done now. I appreciate your help." She was kneading bread. "You can plant a new field somewhere else now." Big Henry got mad. September hadn't counted on that. She figured he would be glad to be cut loose now that she was drying up. She had never thought farmers gave two hoots about the soil or even the harvest once the accounts were settled and the checkbook balanced. She was wrong about Big Henry. He yelled until the windows shook in their sashes. He heaved his huge body against the wall until it cracked. The Peas sucked their thumbs, something they hadn't done for a year. And Root howled.

"OK, OK," September said. She sighed and felt her name change to October. "Sorry. Settle down. I'll make supper now." She felt cords tightening across her chest, bindings she thought she had left in the wing-backed chair many springs ago.

Now October began to grow old. Her hair turned gray, her skin sagged downward, and her fingers were rough twigs. Weakening winds blew through her cells at night. Her children grew and left her. With each departure, she became lighter and dryer, a leaf fluttering and twisting on its branch. When Root took off, she knew she was November. Big Henry snored by the fire. And she longed to break away, to plunge into winter alone, loose, unbound, free to dream of white, cooling snow.

"Now," November said to Big Henry over breakfast the next morning. She pointed to the waist deep snow, the chickadee working its way around the feeder.

"Now, what?" Big Henry asked, wiping egg yolks up with bread.

"Now I'm December. I thank you, you thank me, and let's be off to find our own ways to rest. We've used each other up, don't you think?" December was sure that the children had been all that held Big Henry to her. Now he would be glad to look for new fields to plow. Nothing but a dried up leaf of a woman on this farm.

But she was wrong again. Big Henry's fist smashed down. The forks and knives jumped to the floor. Then it got very quiet. December was buried under Henry's heavy flesh. It was dark, so dark and, yet, she saw a light deep within her man. It was faint at first, then grew brighter and brighter, pushing every shadow away. And there she saw Henry's bowels working, his big heart beating. Deep within his fat and pumping organs a face began to coalesce, a round white face, with still blue eyes. From those familiar eyes hands reached across time and touched December's cheek. For a moment, her blood stopped in her veins. And then she felt Big Henry's breath warming her skin.

"Call me May," she whispered to her husband.

"I've always wanted to," Big Henry said. His pulse kept time and together they moved, thus, past winter's cold toward the thaw.

ABOUT THE AUTHOR

LB was born 40 years ago in Chicago. As the daughter of a foreign service officer, most of her youth was spent overseas. When she returned to the United States, Washington D.C.'s suburbs seemed the most foreign territory of all. She graduated from Boston University with a degree in Fine Arts, joined VISTA, married Keith Valiquette, and began working with emotionally disturbed children in LaCrosse, Wisconsin. She has devoted the latter half of her life to rooting, having felt the first time she came to the coulee region that she was home. Now she is a teacher, gardener, aunt, and more.